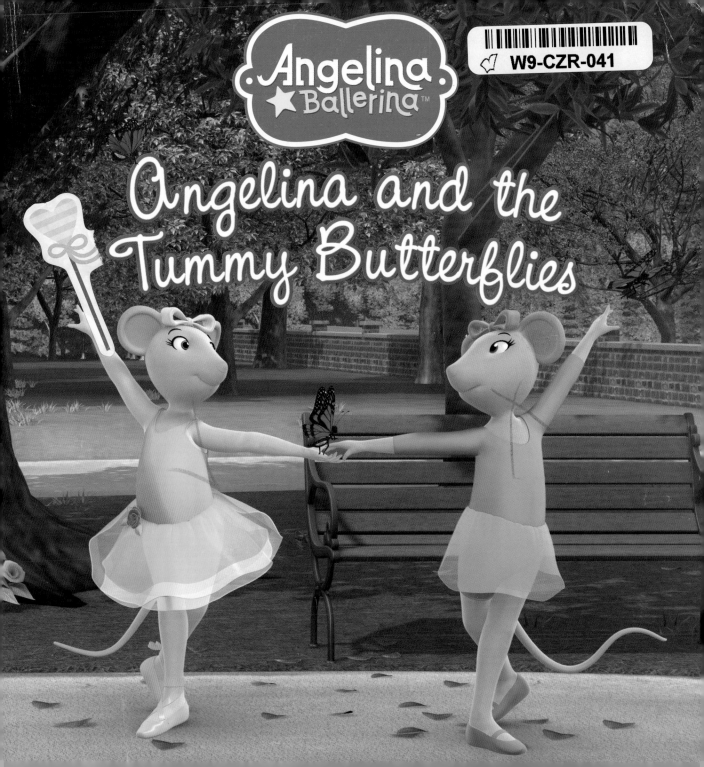

Angelina Ballerina™

Angelina and the Tummy Butterflies

GROSSET & DUNLAP
Published by the Penguin Group
Penguin Group (USA) Inc., 375 Hudson Street, New York, New York 10014, USA
Penguin Group (Canada), 90 Eglinton Avenue East, Suite 700,
Toronto, Ontario M4P 2Y3, Canada
(a division of Pearson Penguin Canada Inc.)
Penguin Books Ltd, 80 Strand, London WC2R 0RL, England
Penguin Ireland, 25 St Stephen's Green, Dublin 2, Ireland
(a division of Penguin Books Ltd)
Penguin Group (Australia), 707 Collins Street, Melbourne, Victoria 3008, Australia
(a division of Pearson Australia Group Pty Ltd)
Penguin Books India Pvt Ltd, 11 Community Centre, Panchsheel Park,
New Delhi—110 017, India
Penguin Group (NZ), 67 Apollo Drive, Rosedale, Auckland 0632, New Zealand
(a division of Pearson New Zealand Ltd)
Penguin Books, Rosebank Office Park, 181 Jan Smuts Avenue,
Parktown North 2193, South Africa
Penguin China, B7 Jaiming Center, 27 East Third Ring Road North,
Chaoyang District, Beijing 100020, China

Penguin Books Ltd, Registered Offices: 80 Strand, London WC2R 0RL, England

Angelina Ballerina © 2013 HIT Entertainment Limited. The Angelina Ballerina name and character
and the dancing Angelina logo are trademarks of HIT Entertainment Limited, Katharine Holabird,
and Helen Craig. Used under license by Penguin Young Readers Group. All rights reserved.
Published by Grosset & Dunlap, a division of Penguin Young Readers Group, 345 Hudson Street,
New York, New York 10014. GROSSET & DUNLAP is a trademark of Penguin Group (USA) Inc.
Manufactured in China.

© HIT Entertainment Limited. HIT and the HIT logo are trademarks of HIT Entertainment Limited.

ISBN 978-0-448-46281-3

HiT entertainment

10 9 8 7 6 5 4 3 2 1

Angelina Ballerina™

Angelina and the Tummy Butterflies

inspired by the classic children's book series by author Katharine Holabird and illustrator Helen Craig

Grosset & Dunlap
An Imprint of Penguin Group (USA) Inc.

One beautiful spring day, Angelina Ballerina and
her best friend Alice were outside dancing and reciting
poems. The next day at school was Poem Day! All the
mouselings were memorizing poems to say out loud to
the whole class.

"Look! A purple butterfly!" Angelina said. "Oooh, I'd love to hold it."

But when she reached out, the butterfly fluttered away.

"Oh no! We scared it off!" said Alice.

But there was no time to be sad. The mouselings had to get to dance class, so off they went together!

On the way to dance class, Alice practiced her poem, but she kept forgetting the words.

"Oh dear. What if I forget the words to my poem when I'm in front of the whole class?" she asked Angelina.

"Don't worry, Alice. I'm sure you'll remember your poem," Angelina said kindly.

When they got to the dance studio, their teacher, Ms. Mimi, was starting a new lesson.

"Today we're going to try some new jazz moves, like the catwalk," she said with a smile.

The mouselings lined up and practiced doing catwalks,
pencil turns, and fan kicks together. They had lots of fun trying
out the new jazz moves!

"Now you can all make up your own dances," said Ms. Mimi.
The mouselings started dancing—all except Alice. Angelina
took her friend's hand and invited her onto the dance floor.

"Come on, Alice! Let's make up a new dance called Jump
Over a Log!" said Angelina, giggling.

Alice began to giggle, too, and soon the mouselings were
twirling and dancing together.

The bell rang. "We'll do more jazz dancing next class," said Ms. Mimi.

"We still have time to practice our poems," said Viki.

Suddenly Alice stopped giggling. "Oh no. What if I forget my poem again?" she wondered nervously.

Instead of going to her next class, Alice went outside. She
was still worried about her poem. She was watching a pretty
purple butterfly flutter around when Ms. Mimi walked over.

"Alice, are you all right?" asked Ms. Mimi.

"My tummy feels funny. I'm afraid I'll forget the words to
my poem in front of everyone," said Alice.

Ms. Mimi pointed to the purple butterfly.

"See this butterfly? It reminds me of how worried I used to get before my performances," Ms. Mimi said.

"Really?" asked Alice.

"Yes. I used to get tummy butterflies," Ms. Mimi explained. "That's when it feels like there are butterflies fluttering inside your tummy."

"That's exactly how I feel, Ms. Mimi. I have tummy butterflies!" said Alice.

After school, Alice told her friends about the tummy butterflies.

"I've had tummy butterflies before!" said Angelina.

"Me too!" said Viki.

When Alice heard that her friends got nervous, too, she felt better. She began to practice her poem again, but as soon as she made a mistake, she gave up!

Angelina saw how upset her friend was, so she took
Alice's hands and spun her around.
"Don't worry, Alice. Let's practice jazz steps instead.
You can try your poem again later," said Angelina.

Viki and Gracie joined in, and soon all the mouselings
were dancing and giggling, including Alice.
"I wish reciting my poem was this much fun!" said Alice.

Later that night, Angelina thought about Alice.
I wish I could take away her tummy butterflies! she thought.

Angelina began to daydream. She thought about the purple butterfly. It gave her a great idea to help Alice! Angelina couldn't wait to tell her friend the next day.

The next day was Poem Day, and Angelina, Viki, Gracie, and A.Z. found Alice practicing her poem by the stage with her eyes shut tight.

"Alice!" they cried.

Alice opened her eyes and saw four beautiful butterflies that her friends had made for her. The mouselings were making the butterflies dance in the air.

"It's time for our butterfly jazz dance!" said Angelina, and she gave Alice a lovely green butterfly.

"For me?" asked Alice. "It's so pretty! Thank you!"

A.Z. turned on the jazz music, and Alice began to dance with her butterfly. All her friends joined in.

After their dance, Angelina led Alice to the front of the stage.

"Now it's time to recite your poem, Alice," said A.Z.

"Right now? But . . . I'm dancing!" said Alice.

"Exactly! I bet you can dance and say your poem at the same time," said Angelina.

Alice said a few words and took a few steps, and soon she was dancing and reciting her poem, with some help from her friends.

When the performance was over, the mouselings clapped and cheered, "Hooray for Alice!"

"I did it! I remembered all the words!" cried Alice.
"We had so much fun dancing, you forgot your tummy butterflies and they disappeared!" said Angelina.

Alice hugged Angelina. Alice was so happy—she had remembered her poem, *and* she had made up a beautiful new dance: the Butterfly Dance!